# SCAMPER

## With the Peanut Butter Feet

## BY
## PATRICIA EYTCHESON TAYLOR

## Scamper, the Mischievous Squirrel: Book 1

Scamper with the Peanut Butter Feet
© 2010 Patricia Eytcheson Taylor

Published by:
Catch-A-Winner Publishing
PO Box 160125
San Antonio, TX 78280
Phone: 210-387-8189
E-mail: info@catchawinnerpublishing.com

ISBN: 978-0-9845630-0-5

Illustrator: Nancy Garnett Peterson

## Other Books

## by Patricia Eytcheson Taylor

**Catch a Winner**
**Catch a Winner Leaves the Ranch**
**Catch a Winner and the Mystery Horse**
**Let's Ride a Texas Horse**
**On the Wings of the Wind: A Journey to Faith**

To: Cole

# Dedication

## To all our grandchildren

Aunt Boo Says
Reading Makes Winners!

Pat Eytcheson Taylor

Scamper was a big gray squirrel who lived in Aunt Boo's yard. At times, Aunt Boo called him sassy because he constantly chattered and always got what he wanted.

Aunt Boo's orchard was filled with special goodies, which Scamper loved to eat. There were sweet red apples, juicy purple plums, and tasty pecans.

Scamper was never satisfied. He wanted all the goodies, especially the yummy golden cornbread Aunt Boo baked for the birds every morning.

Scamper, with a pot belly full,
plopped down on the old stone wall.
His eyes were shut, but he was not
sleeping. He was thinking about
what his next move would be.

Suddenly, Scamper came alive with his eyes wide open, and his tail flashed. He jumped down from the wall and scampered off to Aunt Boo's favorite pecan tree.

Scamper ran up the hole in the old tree, where he was still able to keep an eye on everything going on in Aunt Boo's yard. Then he spotted some tempting pecans out on the limb. He swished his big bushy tail and swatted the nuts until they fell to the ground. Scamper took them one by one back to his hideaway in the old pecan tree where he sometimes slept.

When Scamper completed storing his
nuts in the hole of the tree, he thought
he would venture over to the bird feeder.
No birds were in sight. Scamper jumped
from the tree and grabbed onto the bird
feeder. There was no sign of cornbread or
even crumbs left.

Scamper flashed his tail and took off across the yard to Aunt Boo's house, chattering all the way. Aunt Boo could hear him coming. She looked out her kitchen window and saw Scamper hanging on the tree and looking right at her! He watched every move she made. Aunt Boo knew what Scamper wanted.

Scamper had spotted a fresh pan of warm golden cornbread sitting on her kitchen table. His nose twitched and his tail flashed. The scent from the cornbread drove him crazy. There was nothing like Aunt Boo's delicious golden cornbread. Now he wanted the cornbread she baked for the birds. Something had to be done!

"Whose yard is this?" asked Aunt Boo. "Scamper's or mine?"

Aunt Boo was in deep thought. How was she going to keep Scamper away from the cornbread she baked for the birds? She thought and thought as she laid the cornbread in the bird feeder. She didn't know that Scamper, with his eyes as big as saucers, was in the treetop watching her every move. Aunt Boo returned to the house. She looked out the window to be sure that Scamper did not get the cornbread.

There was Scamper sitting in the bird feeder eating away.

Out the door Aunt Boo went, this time carrying a dish towel with her.

"Shoo, shoo, Scamper," Aunt Boo yelled.

Suddenly, a gust of wind blew the dish towel out of Aunt Boo's hand, and it landed on Scamper's head.

Bewildered, Scamper shook his head as the towel fell freely to the ground. He jumped to the nearest tree, where he peeked out at Aunt Boo.

"So you think you are smarter than me, do you?" Aunt Boo said as she grinned. "Well, we will see about that."

Aunt Boo went back to the house, and Scamper returned to the bird feeder and her cornbread. He nibbled as fast as he could, but he kept a watchful eye out for Aunt Boo.

Scamper was not taking any chances. He thought he was too smart to be caught.

Aunt Boo sat down in her rocking chair on the patio, watching Scamper as he peeked out from behind the tree. "Oh, what should I do? Oh, what should I do?" she said to herself.

She shook her finger at him. "You naughty boy. What am I going to do with you?"

Scamper stayed behind the tree. He could see Aunt Boo shaking her finger at him.

The birds returned to the bird feeder, but Scamper was not going to let the birds have his share of the cornbread.

"No, sir. It is mine, too," said Scamper to himself.

Scamper jumped again, this time straight out. He landed right in the middle of the feeder, feet first, causing the birds to scatter all over the yard.

It was time. Time for Aunt Boo to put her plan into action. She went to her food pantry where she took off the shelf a jar of peanut butter and a box of crackers.

"This will do," she said.

Aunt Boo spread peanut butter on the crackers, and then off she went with the crackers and the jar of peanut butter. She smeared a big glob of peanut butter on the bottom of the bird feeder and put the peanut butter crackers in it.

In the meantime, Scamper had left the bird feeder and now was lying flat as a pancake on the tree branch above Aunt Boo's head, watching her at work.

As the delicious aroma of the peanut butter reached Scamper's nose, his chattering became louder and louder. He could not wait to get his paws on the peanut butter crackers.

When Scamper finished the last cracker, he said to himself, "Oh my, that was delicious."

All of a sudden, Scamper could not move. His feet were covered with peanut butter.

Scamper was a total ooey, gooey mess. He tried to lift one foot, but Oh! It was so ooey. Scamper tried to lift his other foot, but Oh! It was so gooey. Ooey, gooey peanut butter was everywhere!

Scamper licked and licked his peanut butter feet and his bushy tail until he was exhausted. By the time he was finished, he did not like peanut butter, and he certainly did not like the sticky bird feeder!

As Aunt Boo watched Scamper from the window, she laughed and laughed! "That will teach you," she said softly. "Now you will leave the bird feeder alone!"

"But," she promised, "you will have a
feeder of your very own." After all,
Aunt Boo loved all the birds and the
animals.

Aunt Boo kept her word. She made a feeder just for Scamper, filling it with red apples, juicy purple plums, crunchy nuts, and her delicious golden cornbread.

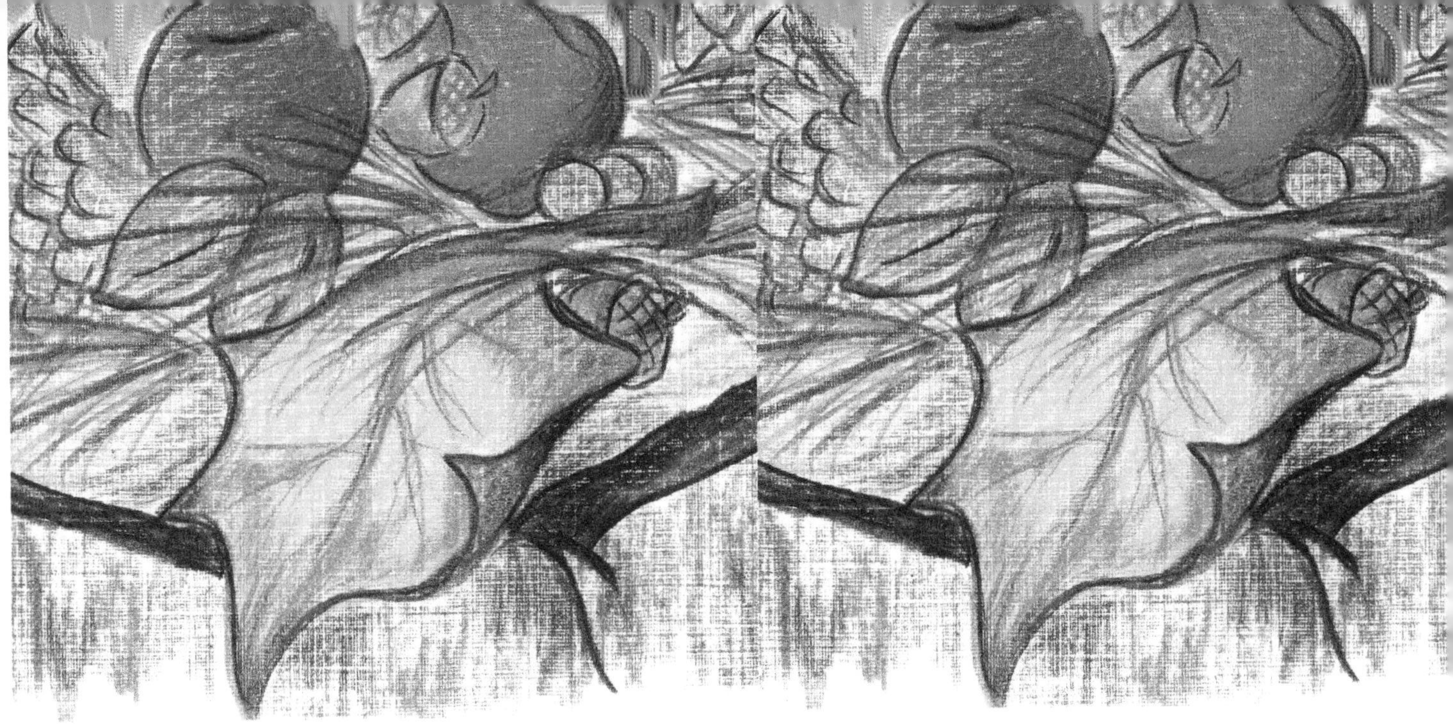

To this very day, Scamper still lives in Aunt Boo's yard, where he is a happy, sassy squirrel, but still mischievous.

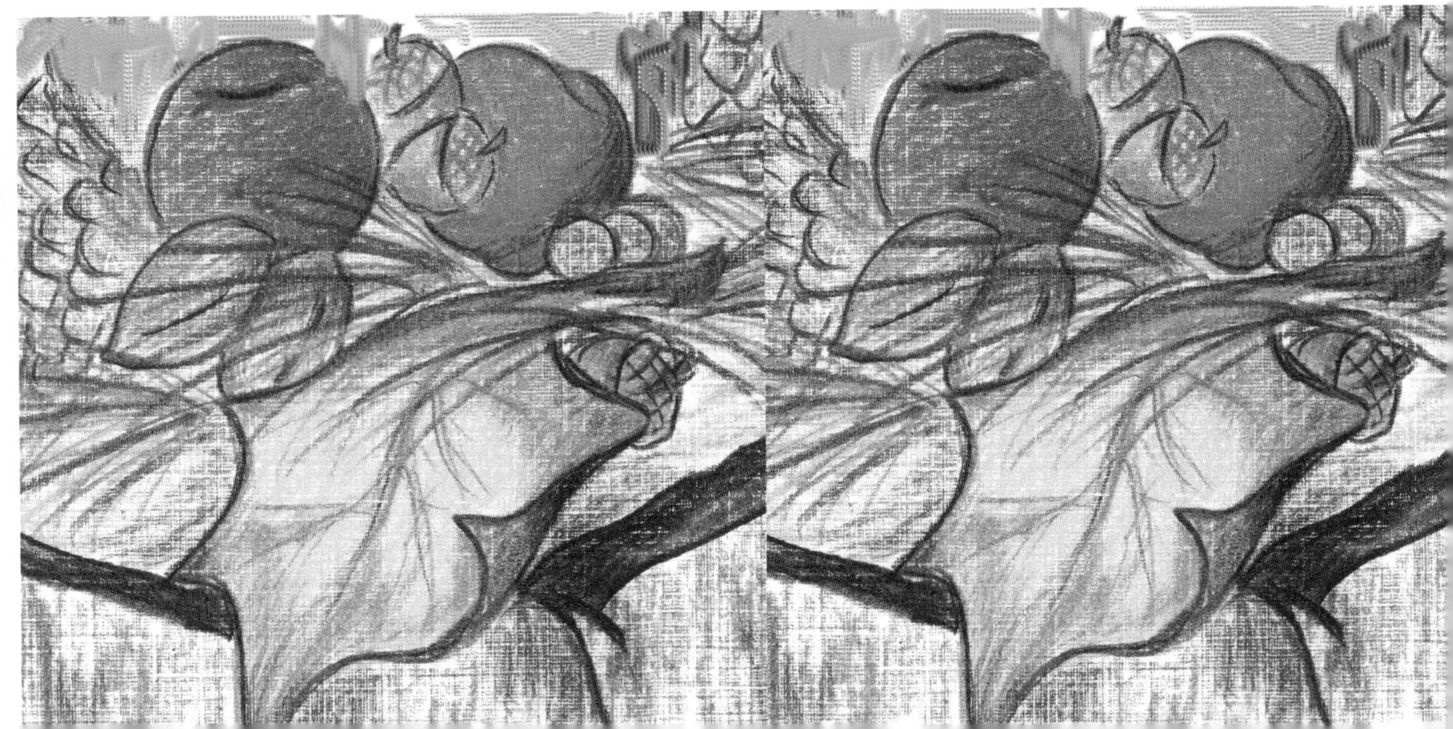

Follow the adventures of Scamper, the Mischievous Squirrel in Book 2. He continues to torment Aunt Boo, and he hides his nuts in the trees and the yard. He finds the perfect place to hide them to his pleasure, but not Aunt Boo's.

Coming in Fall 2010.

Author Patricia Eytcheson Taylor

# About the Author

Patricia Eytcheson Taylor met her first husband, John, on the beaches of southern California, where she grew up. Her mother was very ill, and her father made sure she had plenty of animals to give her love and comfort. Pat learned to understand and communicate with the animals, making it easy for her to tell their stories when she became a writer. Pat and John came to Texas, where they built a business and raised a family. She wrote three acclaimed children's books about the horse Catch a Winner. After being widowed for several years, she married the Reverend James C. Taylor, an Army chaplain, and together they co-authored a Christian living book, *On the Wings of the Wind*.

# About the Illustrator

Nancy Garnett Peterson grew up in rural Idaho with four brothers, a few acres, lots of chores, and plenty of animals. Her creative talents spring from those early childhood memories and wanting to steal a moment to draw. She studied art at Boise State University and went on to have five children's books published. Humble, Texas, is home for her and her husband, but she ventures back to the Rocky Mountains often for a relaxing dose of the West and hugs from her four granddaughters.

LaVergne, TN USA
31 October 2010
202862LV00002BA